Glimpse

Daniel P. Douglas

ISBN: 978-0997329223

Geminid Press, LLC, Albuquerque, New Mexico

It is part of my responsibility as Commander in Chief of the Armed Forces to see to it that our country is able to defend itself against...

Any possible aggressor...

- President Truman regarding his decision to develop the hydrogen—or super—bomb.

IN DARKNESS, an aged, worrisome married couple rested by a sturdy door in a cramped bomb shelter built for just a few many decades ago during the 1950s.

"Do you think it's safe?" Therese said. Her shaky voice resonated against concrete and metal coldness.

"Safe or not, we have to leave," Liam—her husband of fifty years—said, coughing "Air's no good no more."

Therese reached out and grasped Liam's hand. "What do you think we'll find?"

Living in the shadows had whitened their skin. Despite the dimness, Liam perceived his wife's face. It bore the expression of a mother who long ago realized her children were among the dead. He kissed Therese's forehead, and then said, "Can't be sure about anything. We'll just take it one step at a time."

Therese nodded. "Maybe help has arrived?"

In the darkness, Liam wiped a tear from his cheek. "Only one way to find out."

"I love you, Liam."

"I love you too, sweetheart."

"No matter what waits for us out there…"

"At least we'll have each other."

Liam's crooked fingers found the slack battery in the overhead light fixture and pressed. The battery clicked into place and the bulb above it flickered on.

The pair's timeworn faces flinched and their eyelids danced. Soon, their wrinkled hands joined together on the secure door's wheel-like handle. Only through their combined feeble strength did they succeed in turning the beast.

And in so doing, a vertical sliver of pallid illumination expanded in their midst…

<> <>

Washington, DC, 1949

SEVERAL PEOPLE FILLED the dim, smoke-filled conference room. The most important of them sat around an imposing table. Others of less stature assembled in shadowy concealment behind them.

"Quite by chance, Mr. President, scientists at Los Alamos have cracked a secret out of the recovered technology from the four crashes," a lieutenant general said. His three stars entitled him to a place at the table, of course, but not next to President Truman.

His reference to the four crashes held classification as follows:

```
TOP SECRET//MAJIC/ELECTRIC FROST EVENTS
1936 - Black Forest, Germany
1941 - Vicinity Cape Girardeau, Missouri
1942 - Coastal Los Angeles, California
1947 - Vicinity Roswell, New Mexico
TOP SECRET//MAJIC/ELECTRIC FROST EVENTS
```

Scoffing erupted at the table in response to the general's comments, complete with a Bavarian accent. "Quite by chance. Huh. We've been at this for quite some time," said a scientist who American forces had snatched up in a German research lab during the waning days of World War II. His chair sat a few removed from the President.

The three-star cleared his throat before continuing. "Under sufficient power, sir, a synthesizing device in the electro-magnetic and gravitational propulsion systems can... Can—"

The German scientist cut him off. "Can be deployed to create a fissure—"

"Perhaps a window is a better term?" the three-star said.

"Fine," the former Nazi scientist said.

"Its properties provide a view," the three star said.

Steady, unruffled Talbot, a civilian in his fifties who occupied a spot right next to President Truman, said, "Some refer to it as a 'glimpse,' Mr. President."

"Thank you, Mr. Talbot," the former haberdasher who dropped the atomic bomb, said.

"It provides a view into future space-time awareness," the general said, not wanting to miss out on a possible complimentary annotation too.

But, the German scientist headed off any opportunity of it— slim that it was anyway—when he said, "There's a preliminary run-up period that provides rough location, size, scope, and duration data."

"Giving us time to position assets," added the general without missing a beat.

"And the Russians too, no doubt," the calm Talbot said.

"Your branch will handle *that* as always, Mr. Talbot," President Truman said. Solemn silence gripped him and the room. He peered at the faces around the table, most of which appeared anxious. Feeling the same, the President said, "Is it dangerous?"

The three-star hesitated, then said, "Doesn't seem so." His voice wavered.

"No, no..." the German scientist said. His eyes and bottom shifted side-to-side.

The President's contemplative gaze found the tranquil Talbot, who said, "What we glimpse *could* be dangerous, I suppose."

"How so?" Truman said.

"Depends on what we see, and how we interpret it," Talbot said. He paused, and then added, "And what we decide to do about it."

The President nodded and said, "There is nothing new in the world except the history you do not know."

A subdued chorus of, "Yes, Mr. President," arose around him.

"Or, apparently, the future you do not know," the President said.

◇ ◇

Santa Fe, New Mexico, Late February 1950

COUNTERESPIONAGE TYPES in the know referred to Makar by his code name, "*Calabacita*." They had discovered his suspected activities only of late, and had christened him such because they hoped to squash him one way or another. And the sooner, the better.

A lit cigarette rested in an ashtray beside Makar, who sat alone at a booth near the exit inside a restaurant of old-world charm that served authentic New Mexican dishes. He much preferred red chile on his fare, but made an exception for green chile stew, which he enjoyed at present.

A lone bespectacled customer with unkempt hair sitting elsewhere finished his meal and paid. He stroked his lengthy gray beard and smiled at the gracious waitress as she gathered his payment.

Makar continued to spoon up his stew when the bespectacled customer, while exiting, plopped a small envelope onto the seat next to him. Without interruption to savoring the flavorful blend of spices mixed with pork, green chile, potatoes, onions, and bell peppers, Makar's free hand retrieved the covert message and concealed it among his warm outerwear piled beside him.

Makar decoded and read the information later. The note's few simple phrases about significant increased power needs in a particular building at Los Alamos and interest in the Four Corners region told him all he needed to know.

◇ ◇

Northern Virginia, Late February 1950

UNDER DUSKY GRAYNESS, dense snow crunched beneath Knox's boots as he lumbered closer to a pond's still, dark waters. His deliberate pace appeared cautious, as if he watched for land mines.

Knox's crew cut and mid-thirties age indicated to most people that he had likely served his country in the "Big One," World War II. People's assumptions stood correct, although never confirmed by Knox. He didn't discuss his service, not even with his wife, and he forbade his young son from playing "Army" with the neighbor boys.

The pond's slushy, frigid water floated mere inches from a bench on which the always-relaxed Talbot sat. The sky could be falling all around Talbot and there he would remain, seemingly half-asleep.

Knox found Talbot's tracks and followed them the rest of the way to the bench. The crunch of snow creeping up behind him prompted Talbot to speak. "Last time I saw you, Knox, you were worrying about how the Russians were coming or some such nonsense."

"It's my job to worry," Knox said, brushing away snow from the bench before sitting beside Talbot. "Yours too."

"I miss the ducks," Talbot said, placing his bag of bread slices aside. "I worry about where they've all ventured off to. Think they know something we don't?"

Knox gave the empty pond, then Talbot, a curious glare. "They're in their dens where it's fucking warm."

"I don't think it's called a den."

"I don't—"

"I'm not sure. Maybe roosting place?"

"I don't care."

"Then why mention it?"

"You did."

"I brought up my concern for their whereabouts, yes. But you mentioned the den, carrying forth the conversation, suggesting you held interest."

Knox restrained his frustration best he could.

"You always manage to give me a chuckle, Knox. I appreciate that. God how I appreciate that."

"You don't make me laugh," Knox said.

"No. But I do make you work. And you seem to like that." Talbot paused and regarded Knox carefully before saying, "The doctors say the work and their prescribed remedies are good for you."

Knox offered a subdued nod and grunt. "Where is it this time?"

"Preliminary data indicates New Mexico. You been to the tailor?"

"Yes."

"And the others?"

"Working on it."

"Good. Good."

"Not sure this dark, identical look is the way to go."

"And yet the bosses have decided. It will help to confuse and frighten they say."

"Saying it doesn't make it true. And holding a higher pay grade doesn't mean you're smarter."

Talbot offered a knowing nod. "Time will tell on the new uniforms. In the meantime, they'll be very slimming if anything. Besides, truth isn't what people really want."

Knox pondered the gray clouds for a moment before saying, "Los Alamos, then?"

"At first. And as such, do anticipate a certain level of understanding from our primary adversary." Talbot withdrew an envelope from his coat and handed it to Knox.

"Place needs a better plumber," Knox said, tucking the envelope away.

"Yes, some scientists do love to share knowledge," Talbot said, sighing. "You have authority to address wayward individuals outside the fence line as needed."

A far off stare met Talbot's reference to Russian infiltrators and their support network external to lab property.

"From Los Alamos," Talbot said, "you'll head to parts northwest for an aerial glimpse."

Knox inflicted another curious glare at Talbot.

A half smile curled up on Talbot. "And allegedly, it's much more than the Russians who we anticipate catching sight of this time."

Knox lit up a cigarette while he contemplated the subtext of Talbot's words. "Truman's special group divining celestial messages again?"

Talbot retrieved his bread slices, tucked them away, and then stood. His gaze drifted out over the empty pond and beyond. "I do hope the ducks are okay."

"Perhaps all this debate about building the super frightened them off to somewhere safe from thermonuclear vaporization."

Talbot chuckled and peered down at Knox. "See. You make me laugh yet again. With the super, nowhere will be safe."

◇ ◇

Farmington, New Mexico, March 15, 1950

AN HOUR EARLIER inside the cut-rate motel room, Knox had opted for an upright nap in a beige upholstered chair with dried stains of various shades. He had chosen this over resting on the bed, which also held its own share of stains.

Knox twitched. Subconscious war horrors provoked him. His face contorted. He heard battle shouts and clamor rise in his head: Soldiers ran, his own hastened breathes, the whistle of incoming artillery shells, orders to take cover, explosions, the zip of a German MG-42 machine gun, men dying…

Knox jerked awake, out of breath.

A knock on the room's thin wood door finished its quick rapping.

Knox stood in haste and—lightheaded from rising too fast—gripped the chair to gain stability. The knock rattled again.

"Hold on," Knox said.

He straightened his stylish black suit, white shirt, and black tie. A quick glance at the table confirmed his fashionable black hat and sunglasses remained nearby.

On his way to the door, he spotted himself in a mirror. He halted, looked himself up and down. "Men in black," Knox said, mumbling. "That's what they'll call us."

Answering the door, he found two of his associates—Giles and Cobb—standing outside. Both wore the new black attire required by higher authority.

Well, sort of...

"The box?" Knox said, stone-faced and subdued.

"Under lock and key and right nearby," Giles said, shoving a thumb at the motel's parking lot where a panel van sat nearby.

Knox spotted the van. Then, his gaze drifted toward the sky. The pair on his doorstep noticed. They followed Knox's lead, and peeked upward, uncertain.

Nothing but empty blue sky stretched above them.

Moments later, Knox locked the door and turned to the men who now stood inside his room. His eyes inspected Giles first. "Nice suit," he said.

"Custom made to my gorgeous specifications," Giles said.

"Uh-huh," Knox said, moving on to Cobb. The man held a shit-eating grin. Knox returned the gesture. "Not sure what to do right now," he said, examining Cobb in his black, priestly garb. "Part of me feels compelled to kneel before you and ask for Godly forgiveness. The other part—which is mostly comprised of my right hand and its trigger finger—feels compelled to grab my forty-five and unload on you."

"Suit wasn't ready," Cobb said, in a southern drawl. "Borrowed the next best thing. My cousin's man-of-the-cloth garb. All black but for this here white fleck thing at the collar."

"Could represent a separation of church and state issue if you ask me," Giles said.

"And yet no one did," Cobb said, getting in Giles's face. "I improvised. At least I'm smart enough to do that."

"Stop," Knox said, intervening. "Cobb?"

"Yes, my son?"

"Go somewhere in this podunk town and buy something off the rack. I don't care if it's black, white, pink or green. Just get yourself in a fucking suit. And may the good Lord have mercy on your wretched soul."

"Thy will be done," Cobb said, bowing out toward the door.

Giles reached for a newspaper on the table and started reading it.

"And make it quick," Knox said, lighting up a smoke. "We've got an aerial glimpse coming."

Giles and Cobb halted their actions. They both noticed how Knox's hand trembled when he took a drag off the cigarette. The pair exchanged concerned glances before going on about their business.

Neither one of them had ever seen Knox tremble before.

MAKAR PEERED AROUND the ragged interior of an abandoned, dilapidated storehouse on the outskirts of town. The aged structure stood adjacent to railroad tracks and amid bare deciduous trees. An unopened portable radio set waited for his use on the floor next to him. It looked like a sturdy suitcase.

A gratifying sense of nostalgia gripped Makar. The place reminded him of his *glorious* role in the defense of Stalingrad. How he had loved killing Germans. And Russian *cowards* who fled from battle. The clamor of a passing train rattled the building some, but this just seemed to please him even more.

Stepping up to a blemished window that held no promise of budging open, Makar opted for the next best way to view the outdoors from its location. He retrieved a short segment of sturdy metal pipe from the grubby floor and smashed away the window's upper portion of tarnished glass.

Blue sky now revealed itself. Satisfied with his work, he tossed the pipe aside and dusted off his hands. After Makar lit up a cigarette, he used a pair of binoculars to aid his unsullied view out the window.

Other perimeter windows still awaited Makar's special touch. Once he tended to them, he expected their gaps would further contribute to him witnessing reported American technological advances first hand.

◇ ◇

COBB FOUND what he sought in a nearby thrift store. Not quite black, charcoal gray would have to do. Approaching the counter to pay, he cast an eyeball on the barely twenty-year-old *stacked* clerk with a *classy chassis*. Cobb felt sympathetic—among other things—for the *hottie* who seemed to endure with all the politeness in the world a shopper named Betty, a white haired intermeddler who sang about some strangeness "Chuck and the boys had just seen up in the sky."

"Oh my," the clerk said.

Her sexy, breathy voice aroused Cobb's interest in her even more.

"Could be the Reds, if you ask me," Betty said.

And yet, no one did, Cobb thought.

Noticing Cobb, the clerk grinned and excused herself from Betty, who furrowed her brow at him. "Good afternoon, Father," the clerk said.

"My child, good afternoon to you as well," Cobb said, ignoring Betty. His voice resonated with divine wholesomeness.

"Have you seen 'em?" Betty said, ensuring her place in the conversation.

Cobb regretfully withdrew his gaze from the clerk and peered at Betty's durable features. "I'm sorry, I don't know to what you refer kind ma'am." Cobb tilted his attention to the clerk before he even finished speaking to Betty.

"The silvery discs," Betty said.

Cobb's eyes bulged. But a soldier's discipline kicked in quick, restraining his reaction. He aimed his poised features at Betty. "Discs?"

"Folks are seeing some buzzing around," Betty said, pointing up.

"You don't say?" Cobb paused while Betty nodded, and then he added, "Well, have you seen them?"

Betty shook her head no.

Cobb smiled at the clerk. "And you, child?"

"Oh no. I don't know what I'd do if I saw such a frightful sight," the clerk said, trembling. She laid her hands on the counter.

Cobb leaned in, resting one of his hands on hers, and enjoying the sight of her cleavage in the process. "There, there.

Perhaps it's merely the good Lord blowing leaves about. Or maybe tufts of harmless desert milk weed."

Betty rolled her eyes.

"Or," Cobb continued, "the planet Venus. I believe *even* I glimpsed that heavenly sight on my drive into town today."

The clerk relaxed under Cobb's persuasion. He smiled again at her, and then he peered at Betty. "Maybe suggest those explanations to folks who see these things. May help to calm fears and lessen any mass hysteria."

Betty narrowed her suspicious gaze on him. "Humph. You stayin' in town long, *Padre*?"

"No ma'am, just passing through. Heading over Tuba City way to do the Lord's good work among the... Among the... Uh..."

"Navajos?" Betty said.

"Yes. The Navajos," Cobb said, smiling.

"That's so sweet," the clerk said.

"Well, when you're called to serve, you go and do the bidding of higher authority wherever guided in the best way you can."

The clerk set free a sigh of love for Cobb's apparent devoted holiness. But Betty just raised a wary eyebrow at him.

After paying for the slightly used dark gray suit and bidding the pair adieu, Cobb sauntered through the thrift store's parking lot to his government sedan. As he propped open the car's door, he noticed the rustle of nearby leaves. His gaze followed them skyward.

And that's when his sight caught hold of something else.

Cobb's features slackened, he swallowed hard. While the wind fluttered the leaves in one direction, his eyes—which peered high above toward the altitude where wisps of cirrus flew—tracked the sky in entirely the opposite direction.

"BEEN MEANING TO ASK. Where's the rest of the team?" Cobb said, back in the motel room with Knox and Giles.

Knox rubbed his eyes and sighed. "Anticipated AOR for this glimpse is larger than past ones. From Dulce to Durango, Shiprock to here, we're spread thin."

"Sounds like the boys in the lab might be getting a little carried away," Giles said.

"Like playing with matches just wasn't enough for some of the kids," Cobb said. "They add a gas can to their fun?"

The flame from Knox's lighter flickered high. He lit a cigarette, sucked in a deep drag, and then exhaled. "Two days, gentlemen, and we'll be done."

Giles and Cobb detected Knox's unusual strain again.

"This one's even got you on edge like no other," Cobb said.

"AOR *and* duration are all unlike past ones," Giles added. "That it?"

Knox clenched his jaw. Staring straight ahead and avoiding eye contact with both men, he said, "Giles. Get on the box. Transmit a spot report to Zenith. Advise aerial glimpse is confirmed and underway. Provide Cobb's initial fine points." He paused, took another drag, exhaled, and then said, "Target attribution unknown."

◇ ◇

Farmington, March 16, 1950

GILES SAT SURROUNDED by radio equipment inside the cramped panel van's rear compartment. The gear hummed and spat out periodic crackle. He concentrated as he listened close to the traffic flowing through the earphones positioned on his head.

It wasn't long before his features intensified as spot reports from other team members concerning airborne phenomena zipped across the radio waves. His face twitched, and then his eyes bulged. He scribbled in haste a note on a paper pad. A map of the U.S. Four Corners region attached to the sidewall nearby drew his gaze. His eyes danced at multiple points around the map. He shook his head in disbelief and expelled a heavy sigh.

An incoming transmission for him jerked his attention. Putting a hand to an earphone, he listened close and nodded his understanding. He scribbled more notes. After finishing, he transmitted a message.

"Affirmative Zenith. Golf One will comply."

◇ ◇

INSIDE THE MOTEL ROOM, Knox sat in the wobbly chair and smoked a cigarette. Behind his faraway gaze, a long-suffering mind wandered down traumatic pathways. The rising ache in his chest—only one of several associated physical symptoms—always accompanied these horrifying journeys. He rubbed the space between his breasts without realizing it.

An empty pill bottle rested on its side on the table beside Knox. The doctors—and their top-secret drugs—supplied by higher authority had seemingly failed to protect him from psychological sorties into a war that had ended almost five years ago. The battles for Knox most certainly still raged on.

He twitched at the explosions rising inside his head. His mouth gaped open and his head shook in fright at the rageful wailing of diving Stukas unleashing their whistling bombs.

Knox shot up a shaky arm to protect himself from the incoming Hell.

"No!" he shouted.

He stood, both arms protecting his head. The abrupt movements helped shake off the demons. He caught his breath and gained control of his limbs.

But anger rose within.

He squashed out the stubby bit of smoldering tobacco in the ashtray, then grabbed and flung it. The cheap brass container full of butts cracked against the wall. It plunged onto the worn carpet, sputtering its burnt out waste like a sick, insignificant contrivance.

A knock on the door jerked Knox's head toward it. Then his sudden concerned features targeted the pill bottle on the table. He concealed it before Giles entered the room, but the ashtray mess remained.

Giles updated Knox on the radio traffic and latest instructions from higher authority. Knox took a deep breath and pondered the information in his subordinate's notes. While Giles waited for a response, he spotted the clutter on the floor.

Knox noticed, and said, "Missed the trash can."

Giles appeared unconvinced.

"Make sure Cobb receives the latest protocol," Knox said, checking his watch. He strode to the door.

"And you?" Giles said, scrutinizing his superior.

Waving the notepaper, Knox said, "Off to check the source of these radio signals Zenith provided."

Giles raised an inquisitive eyebrow. "You want help?"

But Knox closed the door behind him, leaving Giles alone and with no response to his question.

<> <>

ARMED WITH the latest disinformation protocol, Cobb cruised the boulevard in his government sedan probing for targets of opportunity. Intermittent sightings of drivers rubbernecking in their cars—parked and otherwise—undulated anxiousness through him. Increased daylight sightings held too much ambiguity over mission success.

He soon spotted a small crowd gawking and pointing skyward. The group gathered in a parking lot adjacent to street-side businesses. Cobb parked around the corner and casually advanced on foot.

Nearing the collection of muttering sightseers, Cobb took a cleansing breath and then allowed his dark, sunglass-shaded gaze to drift upward.

"Never seen anything like 'em," a postal carrier said.

"Heard someone say it could be milk weed blowing about," a middle-aged businessman said.

Cobb allowed himself a grin at that comment.

"Cotton fuzz is what a cop called it," a young grease monkey said.

Cobb cleared his throat, and then said, "You know gents, when I served in the Office of Naval Research..." He paused.

The momentary lapse achieved the desired result. Folks around Cobb lowered and settled their eyes on him.

"We launched these balloons," Cobb said, continuing. "Called them Skyhook. High altitude research. Very high altitude. Sometimes, they'd fly so high, their envelopes would burst and fragment." The quiet group around Cobb gradually ascended their views again. "Those falling fragments looked a lot like what's up there."

The middle-aged businessman furrowed his brow at the sky, and then peered at Cobb. "A balloon gone to pieces?"

"Just saying," Cobb said, noncommittal. "May be a disintegrating Skyhook." He waited a moment, and then sauntered away, saying, "Y'all have a good day now."

A wake of misgivings rippled behind him.

◇ ◇

THE LATE AFTERNOON SUN draped its dusky rays over a stealthy Knox. On foot, he maneuvered among thick-trunked, barren trees near railroad tracks on the edge of town. Occasional pauses provided him with peeks through petite binoculars. One of those quick looks revealed an antiquated storehouse that appeared vacant.

Hunkering down, he studied the structure and discerned a couple of broken windows. After several minutes, he noticed a familiar sight that prompted an addictive urge within him. What looked like cigarette smoke floated out one of the windows.

Interior darkness failed to reveal a person, but the sight of occasional puffs of fleeting white vapor combined with the knowledge of Zenith's intercepted radio signals confirmed all Knox needed to know.

He allowed his gaze to drift upward, where he squinted into the heights far beyond spindly tree branches. His head tracked the sky, searching…

But he saw nothing.

Settling his sights onto the abandoned storehouse again, Knox heard the low rumbling of an approaching train. He nodded, granting silent permission to himself to proceed on this particular component of his mission.

◇ ◇

Farmington, March 17, 1950

APPREHENSIVE SILENCE overwhelmed Giles and Cobb as they stood next to the panel van in the motel parking lot, gazing upward. The vast intrusion into the clear blue sky and its occasional wispy cirrus far exceeded the boundaries of their unique experiences.

Lowering their heads to gain some relief, both swallowed hard. Their strained sideways glances at each other found shared ashen complexions.

"My God," Cobb said, muttering.

"I should get on the box," Giles said, tugging at discipline from the depths of his core.

Cobb responded with a feeble nod.

"You should get back to delivering your messages, too," Giles said.

Cobb tried to speak, but the words failed to flow from his half-open, dry mouth. After a moment, he shut it in defeat and peered away from Giles, ashamed.

"Pull it together, Cobb."

Staring at the ground, Cobb said, "How can the protocols possibly work against something like that?" His voice trembled.

Giles aimed his view skyward again. Shock restored itself on his face. His eyes panned a vast arc across the heavens. After finishing, he lowered his gaze and found Cobb's anxious features again.

Giles reached way down into his gut for that discipline again. "Lean on your training and just plant the seeds of doubt," he said. "People will choose the prosaic over the profound. History and higher authority will help tend to it. These things will be dismissed, if not long forgotten."

Cobb glared at Giles, his faith still failing him.

◇ ◇

KNOX DROVE his government issued, black Ford sedan with authority and resolution to address the *wayward Calabacita*. But a brief stop for a traffic light interrupted his clear-headed sense.

He spotted several pedestrians gazing skyward, and much more than just curious expressions filled their features. Pain in his chest rose when he saw a little girl with curly hair press against her father's legs. She reached up and clasped his hand with both of hers. Fright maligned her small, innocent features.

Knox swallowed hard. He resisted the urge to glimpse the sight overwhelming the child and the others. Concerned he'd lose his capacity to act, Knox tore his eyes away from the terror-struck girl and focused on the road straight ahead.

He drove on.

Nearing the abandoned storehouse, he parked far enough away to prevent *Calabacita's* discovery of his vehicle. On foot, he again resisted gazing upward, and he maneuvered using the clamor of a passing train to shield the sounds of his approach to the structure.

As expected, puffs of smoke drifted out one of the broken windows. The breach hung on a side of the building opposite to Knox's infiltration. But with the train's ruckus diminishing, he opted for a quick dash across the final, short distance. Taking a quick breath, Knox rushed out from behind the cover and concealment of a thick tree trunk. Upon reaching the storehouse, he pressed his back up against its grimy, timeworn exterior wall near a rickety open doorway.

His next movement was unintended. Just a reflex, really. But having stopped in his new position, Knox the soldier scanned his surroundings. And before he realized it, his eyes shifted skyward, and that's when fear slugged him hard. The unbelievable sight filling the blue above plunged his mind into the war...

In an instant, Stukas rained Hell onto him again. Horrifying death screams resounded in his ears. His fingers clawed into bloody soil in a desperate bid to escape. Shredded body parts hurled through the air and splattered onto the ground around him. Terror-filled faces of his *buddies* gawked at him. Until the dreadful engineering of war obliterated them all from the battlefield and they existed no more...

Knox's eyes danced, and he pressed harder against the wall. His head jerked back and forth. The sudden image of the frightened little girl on the sidewalk appeared to him. She clasped her father's hand and pressed against his leg, seeking his salvation.

Knox sucked in a deep breath, and exhaled.

An inner sense of resolve ignited within the depths of his broken spirit in that moment. And as it propagated and filled his emptiness, Knox established a beachhead on reality again. He gazed upward, clenching his jaw. His gut sank, but he glared in defiance at the vision above.

Tactical, stealthy movements followed. And he penetrated the dim storehouse unseen.

MAKAR GRINNED and felt warm inside as he photographed the sky through a broken window. He had watched the firmament enough to glimpse something that actually evoked a sense of pride and honor. Although still uncertain to what he held witness, *at least it may be Russian*, he had thought.

After snapping a few more photographs, he released his camera. It dangled from his neck by a strap. He blew a chill away from his hands with a few breaths. Stomping his feet for a bit returned circulation to his legs. He lit a cigarette, warmed his hands in his coat pockets, and admired the view again.

The sound of Russian spoken from behind him, however, diminished his moment of satisfaction.

◇ ◇

"I HAVE A MESSAGE from the United States Government," Knox said. He held a large manila envelope in his left hand. His right side and hand angled away from his adversary.

Makar stood upright at the sound of Knox's voice. He released his cigarette and squished it out. After a moment, he responded in his mother tongue. "Your Russian is very good." He sighed, and then turned around. Facing Knox, he said in impeccable English, "But unnecessary since we are in your country and not mine."

Knox stretched out his left arm. Makar's gaze remained steady and level as he withdrew his hands from his coat pockets and retrieved the envelope from Knox.

Before opening it, Makar said, "Have you seen the sky today?"

A subdued grunt acknowledged the question.

The Russian grinned. "There appears to be a red leader among them."

Stone-faced silence met the comment.

"I don't know what it all means," Makar said. "But I do take comfort in that out of hundreds filling the sky, they follow a red leader." Watching Knox's unflinching features, Makar's grin trailed off. He focused on opening the envelope and sliding out a photograph from within it.

And that's when Makar flinched, slight as it was.

The image conveyed that of a suicide. It included graphic details of a certain bearded and bespectacled research scientist with unkempt hair whose brains and bone matter had splattered across a pillow from a single gunshot wound to his temple.

"The pressures of top secret work can lead to rash and lethal behavior," Knox said.

Makar tucked the photograph inside the envelope. He handed it back to Knox, half-smiling.

"You have twenty-four hours to depart my country," Knox said. "Your gear and camera stay, of course." Knox half smiled and stepped back a few.

Makar gazed around at the dilapidated interior. After his eyes finished their journey, he said, "I like this old, worn out building. It reminds me of the war. The defense of Stalingrad. Did you fight in the war?"

Knox stood silent.

"That is fine, you do not have to answer my question." Makar paused. He nodded and said, "You did. I can tell."

"Twenty-four hours, Makar."

The Russian chuckled. "How I miss killing Germans," he said.

Knox tightened his grip on the silenced Colt .45 he held in his right hand. He still angled that side away from Makar.

"But you know what I miss even more?" Makar waited, but Knox remained unresponsive. The spy slid his hands into his coat pockets. "I miss standing over the corpses of cowards who fled from battle."

Knox leaned and raised the Colt just as a gunshot rang out from Makar's right side coat pocket. The next bullet that fired erupted from Knox's barrel.

The round from Makar's pistol missed its target and struck a dense pillar of concrete. Knox's .45 round penetrated Makar's forehead, scrambling a good portion of his brain into mush.

Knox stood over the dead heap, angry and resentful. Another haunting memory poised itself to stalk him.

◇ ◇

Northern Virginia, March 22, 1950

HINTS OF SPRING surrounded Talbot as he sat on the bench by the pond. But still no ducks swam nearby to fetch his bread, which he held bagged up beside him.

Knox strode up behind Talbot, but no telltale snow tracks existed anymore to offer him a safe path to follow. This lack of direction failed to slow his pace, however. In just the few days since he'd run out of his medication, he'd actually felt better and more clear-headed without it.

As he neared Talbot, Knox pulled a newspaper out from under his arm. Sitting on the bench, he offered it to Talbot, who took and unfolded it.

"So nice to see you again, Knox. I look forward to your good humor."

"Have a laugh at that, then," Knox said, gesturing at the paper, which was the *Farmington Daily Times*, dated March 18, 1950. "Nice headline, don't you think?"

"'Huge Saucer Armada Jolts Farmington,'" Talbot said, quoting the front page.

"That followed multiple days of abundant eyewitness sightings of numerous unidentified craft over the city. Thousands of eyewitnesses, Talbot."

"So we've gathered."

"The day I reconciled our differences with *Calabacita* was the armada day." Knox paused and peered toward the sky. "Hundreds, Talbot. They filled the heavens. All led by a red craft." He lowered his head and stared off into the distance. "What did we glimpse?"

Serene Talbot folded up the newspaper and tucked it away. He sighed, and then said, "An armada of flying saucers."

Knox turned and noticed Talbot's empty gaze and pursed lips. "And what else, Talbot? There's more, isn't there?"

Talbot squinted at the trees beyond the pond and said, "A glimpse of things to come. Of course, we don't all agree on what it means. But some fear it. Production of the super has been stepped up. The Russians won't be far behind. Others, many others, will follow suit."

Knox blinked. "What's the estimated date for the… Armada's arrival?" he said.

"You know… As far as the sightings go… Well, mass hysteria and people's imaginations just got the best of them."

"The date, Talbot?"

"Venus. Fragmenting Skyhooks. Blowing leaves and tufts of desert milkweed. Hell. Even illuminated duck bellies."

"Talbot."

"It's all just from so much moonshine too." Talbot gestured as if he drank from a liquor bottle. "It was Saint Patrick's Day, after all." Talbot nodded and chuckled. "More glimpses are planned. Our men in black will be busy and will need many stories to tell. They will confuse, intimidate, and intervene if needed. The glimpses will give us more answers, but people must not know—"

Knox clenched his teeth and swiveled sideways, interrupting Talbot. "When will the armada arrive? And why will it come?" His voice resonated sternness.

Talbot offered nothing but steadfast silence.

Knox stood and marched away.

Talbot peered after him, saying, "Seeing the future doesn't mean you can change it. But you can prepare for it, and survive it just long enough… I hope we can count on you to stay in this."

Knox halted. He sighed, and then said, "What did we glimpse?"

Talbot stood and said, "You know as well as any that humanity's madness is as boundless as it is certain. What did we see? You tell me, Knox. What do you see when you close your eyes at night?"

His heart ached again, so Knox rubbed his chest. He shook his head. "War."

"Prepare for it, Knox, because it will come. Only those who survive long enough will see the light of day."

A breeze swirled past the two, sending ripples across the pond toward its far shore. Knox loosened his black tie, unbuttoned his white shirt at the collar, and brushed dust off his black suit. He put on his dark sunglasses and watched Talbot return to sit on the bench.

Then, Knox walked away, heading home to his wife and son.

◇ ◇

Personal Bomb Shelter, Late March 2050

THE ELDERLY PAIR exited the structure that Liam's Grandfather Knox built one hundred years earlier. After coughing and straining to gain their bearings amid a dusty realm, Liam and Therese raised their faces to what awaited them.

Wrinkled skin slackened as they glimpsed an endless array of saucer shaped vessels darting about in huge formations above a boundless wasteland of thermonuclear destruction spread out before them. Piles of unrecognizable debris, what must have been their neighborhood, littered the smoldering landscape. Above them, a lone, red, glowing saucer halted. Other discs soon joined it. The formation hovered—in silence—while the red leader descended as if preparing to land.

Liam and Therese leaned into each other and clasped their hands. Both sought comfort and salvation in the other. Together, they collapsed to their knees, weeping.

"He was right," Liam said, struggling. "We survived just long enough. He was right… Help has arrived."

About the Author

DANIEL P. DOUGLAS is a U.S. Army veteran who has also served as a senior analyst in the U.S. intelligence community. As a writer, Douglas creates epic tales—of the past, present, and future—with the most unlikely of heroes, and calls upon them to join extraordinary and mysterious struggles. His characters' sometimes-reluctant choices and actions put them on a collision course with destiny and reveal unimaginable truths. In every pulse pounding, edge-of-your-seat adventure, survival means confronting personal flaws and doubts, and forging unexpected fates as inspiring new champions in the eternal battle against evil. Douglas explores this theme through science fiction, action-adventure, conspiracy, mystery, suspense, thriller books and screenplays.

Born and raised in Southern California, Douglas has also lived in Virginia and Arizona. He now lives in New Mexico with his family, pets, and livestock, and enjoys reading science fiction and conspiracy thrillers as much as writing them.

For more information about Daniel P. Douglas, please visit http://danielpdouglas.com.